Anna Carries Water

For all the little water carriers of the world—OS

For my family, with all my love, and for old friends with new babies—LJ

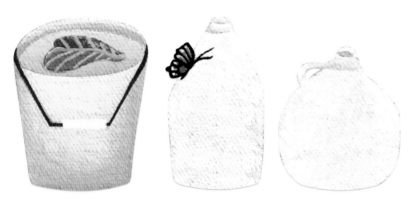

Published by Tradewind Books in 2013. Published in the USA in 2014. Text copyright © 2013 Olive Senior. Illustrations copyright © 2013 Laura James. All rights reserved. No part of this publication may be reproduced, stored in a retrieval system or transmitted, in any form or by any means, without the prior written permission of the publisher or, in the case of photocopying or other reprographic copying, a license from Access Copyright, Toronto, Ontario. The right of Olive Senior and Laura James to be identified as the author and the illustrator of this work has been asserted by them in accordance with the Copyright, Design and Patents Act 1988.

Book design by Elisa Gutiérrez
The artwork was created on canvas and photographed by Janis Wilkins.
The type is set in Liebe Ruth.

Printed and bound in Korea in August 2013 by Sung In Printing Company.

LIBRARY AND ARCHIVES CANADA CATALOGUING IN PUBLICATION

Senior, Olive
    Anna carries water / by Olive Senior ; illustrations by Laura James.

ISBN 978-1-896580-60-9

    I. James, Laura, 1971- II. Title.

PS8587.E552B57 2012   jC811'.54   C2013-901535-3
. . . .

The publisher thanks the Government of Canada and Canadian Heritage for their financial support through the Canada Council for the Arts, the Canada Book Fund and Livres Canada Books. The publisher also thanks the Government of the Province of British Columbia for the financial support it has given through the Book Publishing Tax Credit program and the British Columbia Arts Council.

Canada Council for the Arts   Conseil des Arts du Canada   BRITISH COLUMBIA ARTS COUNCIL

Olive Senior

Anna Carries Water

illustrations by

Laura James

Tradewind Books

VANCOUVER · · LONDON

Anna wanted to carry water on her head.
More than anything.

Her family lived way out in the countryside.
Their water did not come from a tap.

Every evening after school, the children went to the spring for water.
They walked in a straight line:

First Doris then Karen then Rohan then Trevor

then Robbie and last of all far behind came Anna.

When she got to Mister Johnson's field, Anna ran to catch them up.
Anna was afraid of the cows.

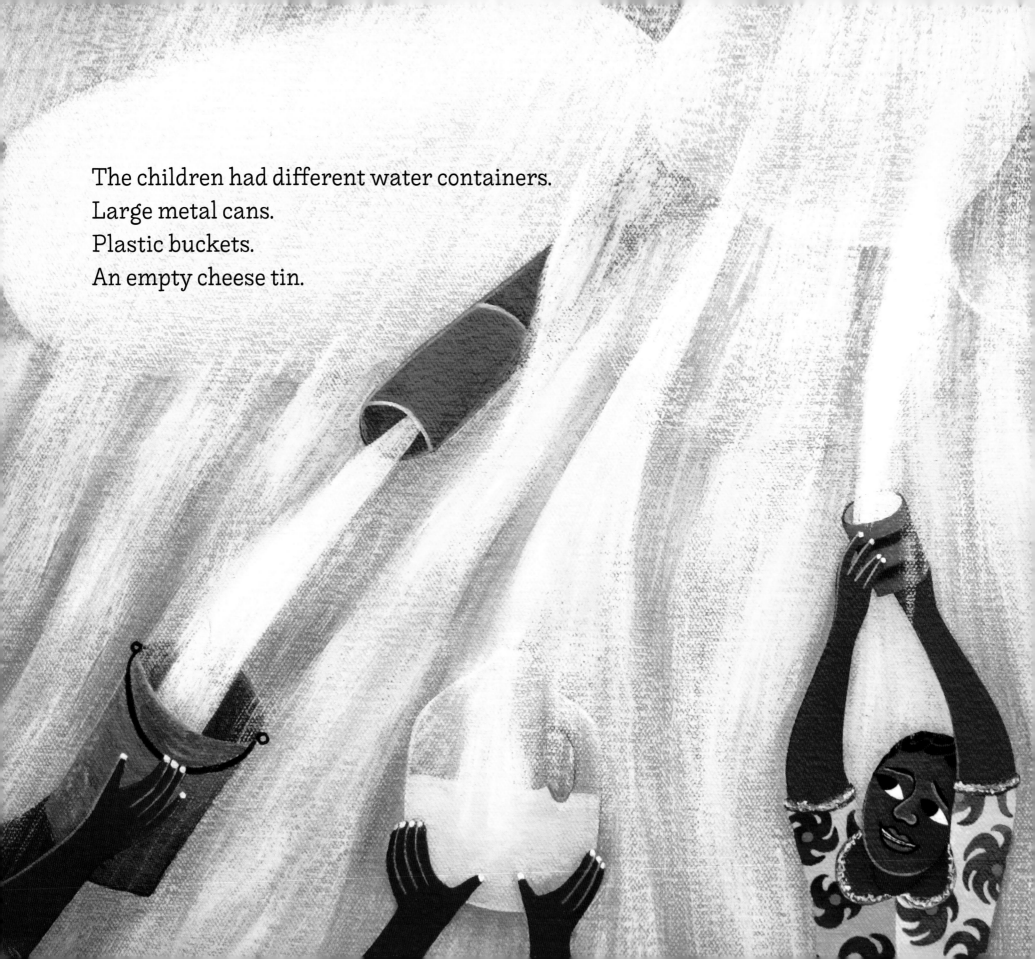

The children had different water containers.
Large metal cans.
Plastic buckets.
An empty cheese tin.

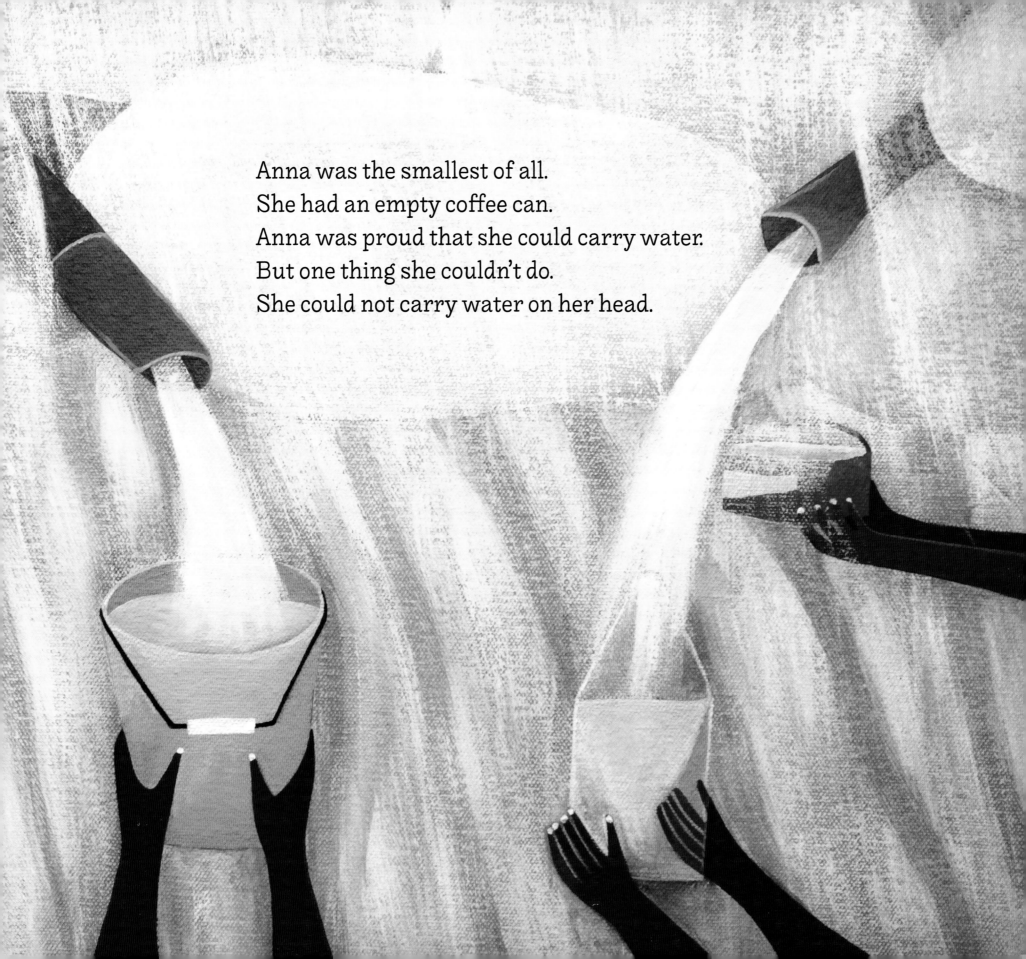

Anna was the smallest of all.
She had an empty coffee can.
Anna was proud that she could carry water.
But one thing she couldn't do.
She could not carry water on her head.

Doris filled her big container first.
She floated a dasheen leaf on top.
Doris walked with her hands at her sides.
Not a drop spilled.
Then Karen filled her bottle. Rohan helped her.
Not a drop spilled.
All the children helped each other.
They stood ready to go.
All except Anna.

They turned to look at Anna.

Anna filled her can with water.

"Come on Anna," Doris said, "just hold it with your two hands."

"No," said Anna, "I want to carry it on my head."

"You will wet up your clothes," said Rohan.

"I won't if I put the leaf in," said Anna.

"Oh Anna," they all said crossly.

Anna picked a dasheen leaf.
She tore a little piece off.
She put it on top of the water so it wouldn't splash.
Anna put the can of water on her head.

The can fell off. Anna got wet.
She started to cry.
"Now see what you have done," said Rohan.
Anna cried harder.
"Don't cry," said Robbie. He filled Anna's can again.
"Hold it with your two hands, Anna.
Don't put it on your head."
"All right," said Anna.

The children walked in a straight line home.
From the spring.
Across Mister Johnson's field.
They carried the water to their house.

Water for cooking and drinking.
Water for washing dishes.
Washing faces.
Cleaning teeth.

And for washing dirty feet at night before putting them into clean beds.
Water for the animals.
They didn't carry water for bathing or washing clothes.
Everyone bathed and washed clothes in the river.

Doris took Anna inside to change her clothes.
Anna was happy again.
But she still wished she could carry water on her head.
"As soon as you are old enough to learn, you will learn," Doris said.
"But how?" Anna asked.
"It just happens," said Karen. "So don't worry."

One day, just like any other day, the children went to the spring.
They filled their containers and put them on their heads.
Anna filled her can and held it tightly.
They set off for home:

First Doris then Karen then Rohan then Trevor then Robbie and

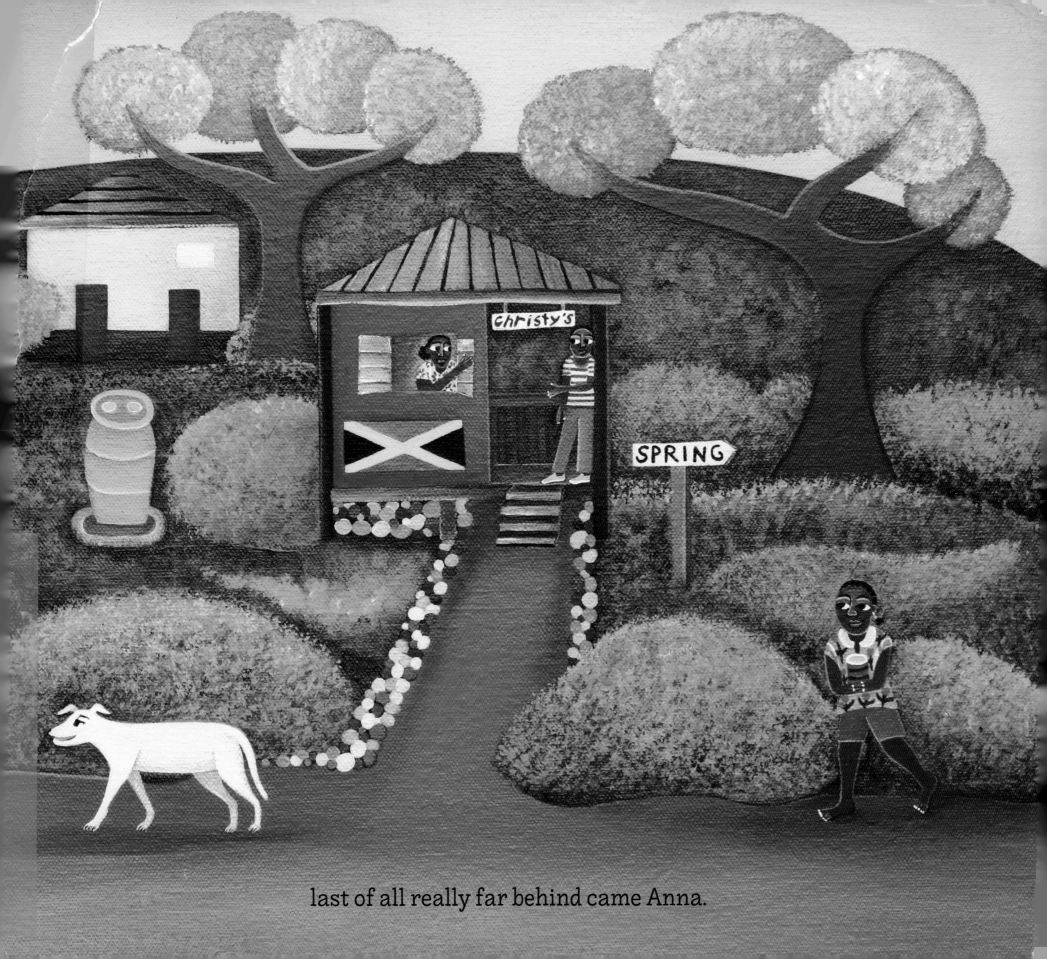

last of all really far behind came Anna.

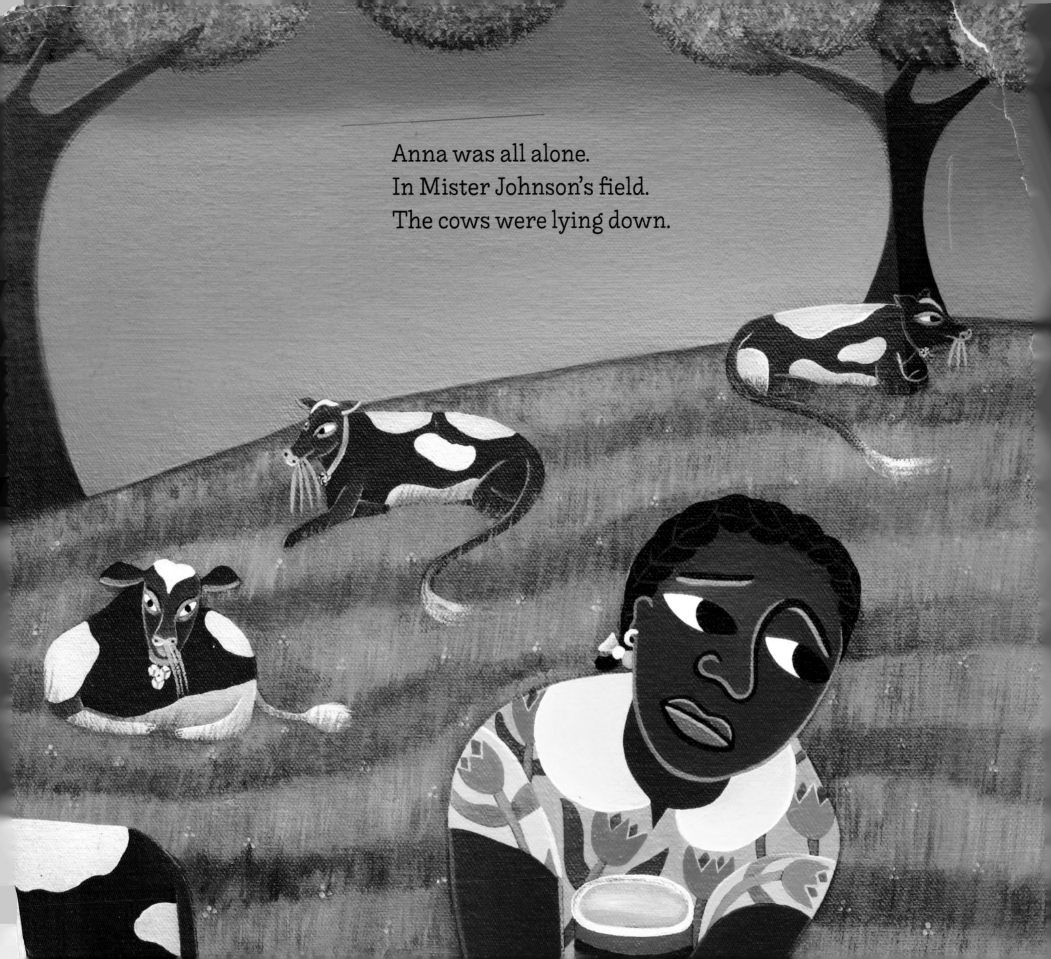

Anna was all alone.
In Mister Johnson's field.
The cows were lying down.

The cows were chewing and chewing.
Anna looked at the nearest cow.
The cow looked at Anna.

Anna was so frightened, she didn't think.
She just took off.
She ran and ran.

Meantime, the others had reached home.
"Where's Anna?" Mama cried.
"Where's Anna?" said everyone.
They all rushed over to Mister Johnson's field.

They couldn't believe what they were seeing.

Anna ran straight up to her mother.
Her father laughed and grabbed the can of water and drank it.
Her mother hugged her.
"Oh Anna, you never spilled a drop," she said.
"We are proud of you," Papa said.
They all shouted, "Hurrah!"

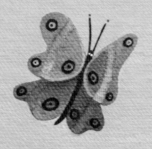

Anna was so happy.
She carried water on her head.
She didn't spill a drop.
She didn't wet her clothes.
She would get a bigger can now.
"Hey," Anna said, "what happened to the cows?"
"What cows?"

"The cows that were chasing me."
"You mean Mister Johnson's lazy cows?" asked Rohan.
They all started laughing.
"Look at the cows, Anna," they said.

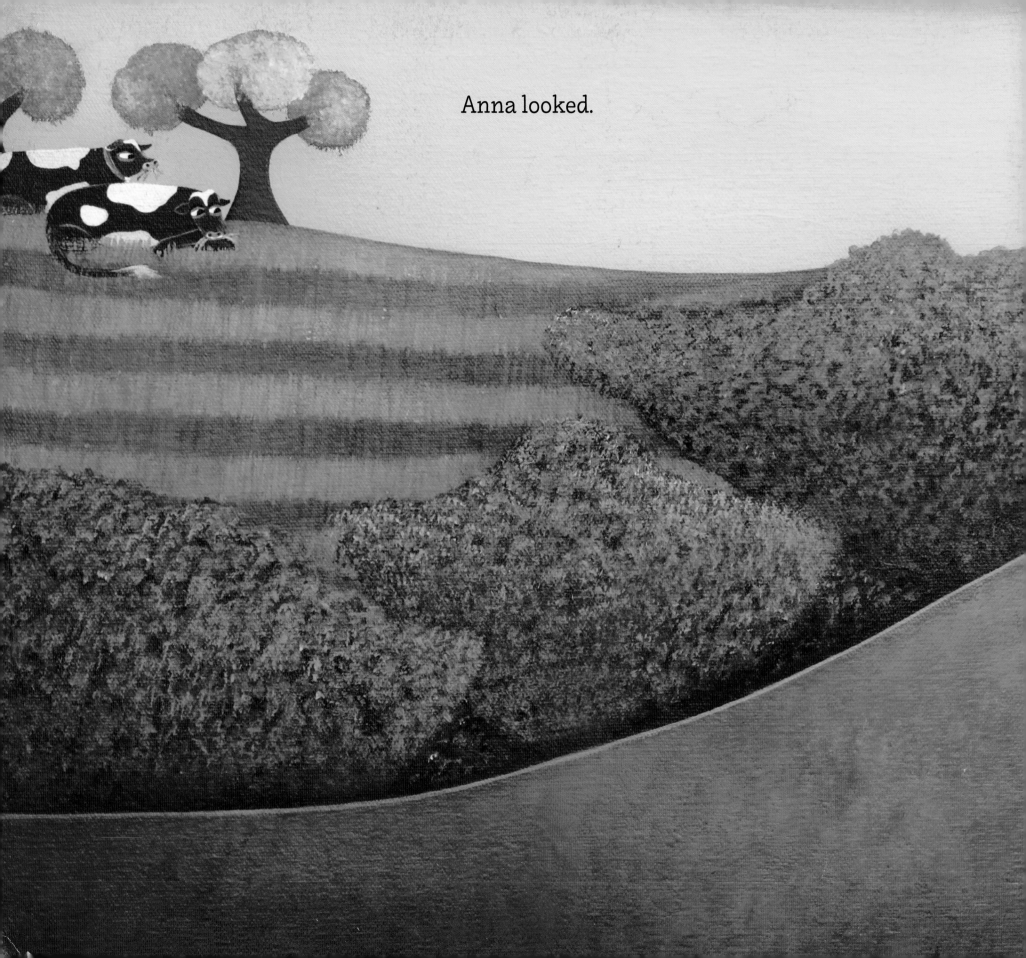

Anna looked.

The cows were lying in the field, chewing and chewing.
Not one had moved.
"Ha ha ha ha ha!" Anna laughed, as loudly as the rest.
She turned cartwheels with happiness.
She didn't feel frightened of anything.

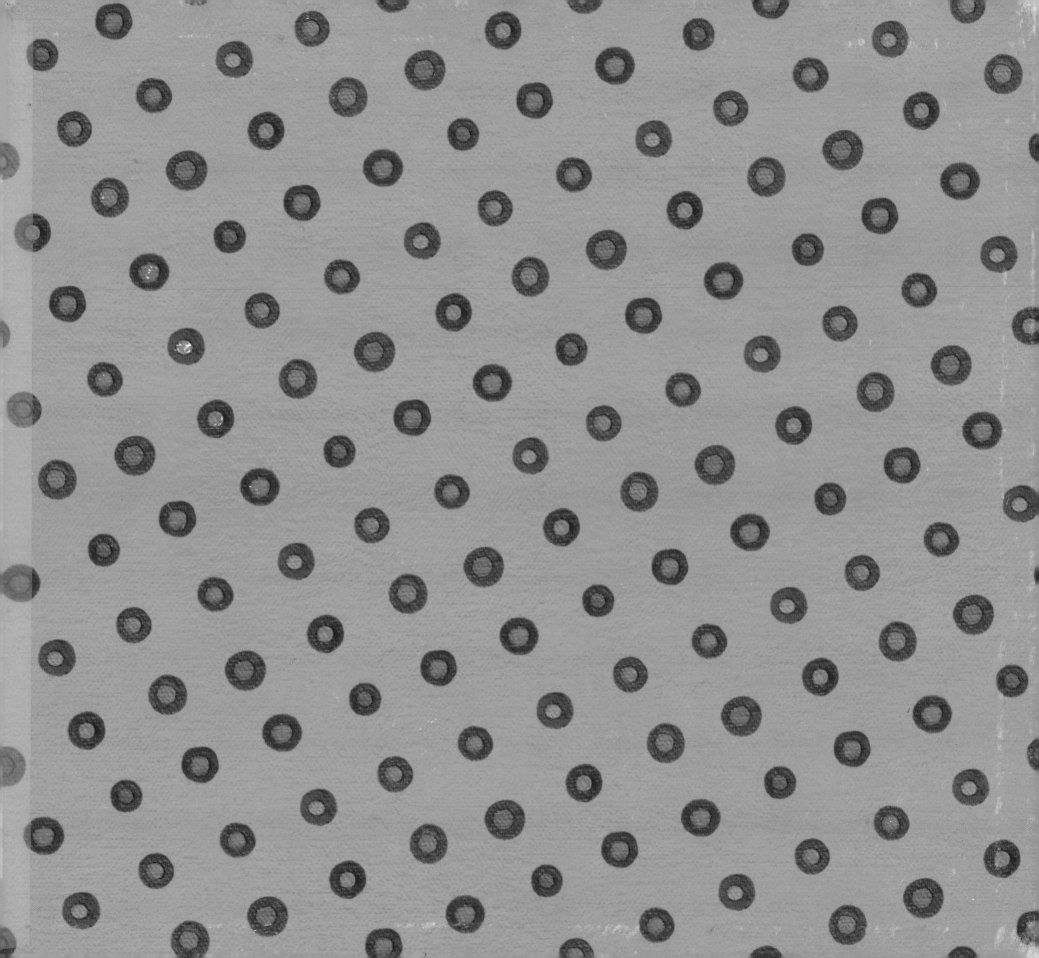